AUSTIN PLAYS FAIR

TONY & LAUREN DUNGY

Illustrations by GUY WOLEK

HARVEST HOUSE PUBLISHERS
Eugene, OR

To our children.
We pray you will find the courage
to honor God in everything you do.
Love, Mom and Dad

Cover design by Kyler Dougherty
Interior design by Left Coast Design

HARVEST KIDS is a registered trademark of The Hawkins Children's LLC.
Harvest House Publishers, Inc., is the exclusive licensee of the federally registered trademark HARVEST KIDS.

AUSTIN PLAYS FAIR

Copyright ©2018 by Tony Dungy and Lauren Dungy
Published by Harvest House Publishers
Eugene, Oregon 97408
www.harvesthousepublishers.com

ISBN 978-0-7369-7324-3 (hardcover)

Library of Congress Cataloging-in-Publication Data

Names: Dungy, Tony, author. | Dungy, Lauren, author.
Title: Austin plays fair / Tony and Lauren Dungy.
Description: Eugene, Oregon : Harvest House Publishers, [2018] | Summary:
   Austin loves everything about football except losing, so when Bryce urges the team to
   tuck their flags so they cannot be taken, Austin agrees although he knows it is wrong.
Identifiers: LCCN 2017038064 (print) | LCCN 2017047656 (ebook) | ISBN
   9780736973281 (ebook) | ISBN 9780736973243 (hardcover)
Subjects: | CYAC: Football—Fiction. | Fairness—Fiction. | Conduct of life—Fiction.
Classification: LCC PZ7.D9187 (ebook) | LCC PZ7.D9187 Aus 2018 (print) | DDC [E]—dc23
LC record available at https://lccn.loc.gov/2017038064

PRINTED IN CHINA
18 19 20 21 22 23 24 25 26 / IM / 10 9 8 7 6 5 4 3 2 1

Austin loved playing football. He loved running down the field, catching passes, and throwing spirals.

But there was one thing about playing with the Trentwood Tigers Austin did *not* like!

The Trentwood Tigers had lost six games in a row.

"Don't worry," said Austin's dad.

"You just need a little more practice."

"Have fun!" said Austin's mom.

"Having fun is more important than winning."

Austin tried to have fun as the Tigers warmed up for their next game, but he still wished the Tigers could win at least once!

Coach Tony blew his whistle. "Okay, Tigers, huddle up!" he called, and the team obeyed.

"We know the Grantville Gators are a tough team," said Coach Lauren.

"And we may have lost a few games lately," said Coach Tony. "But what do we do when we lose?"

Get up, get over it, and try again!" yelled the Tigers.

Coach Tony smiled. "That's right! So let's get out there!"
With a last thumbs-up, the coaches headed for the sidelines.

"Hey, guys," said Brice when the coaches were gone. "I know a trick that can help us win!"

The team exchanged excited looks. "What is it?" asked Carson.

"Tell us!"
begged Jaden.

"Tuck your flag in, like this." Brice showed them his flag belt. "Now the other team can't get it!"

Keiko frowned. "That's not allowed."

Brice wasn't listening. He tugged on his flag. "See? Even if they catch up to you, they won't be able to take it!"

Austin's stomach felt funny. "But that's cheating!"

Brice shook his head. "My brother says everyone does stuff like that. Aren't you tired of losing?" he pleaded.

The Tigers looked at each other. "Well, if everybody does it..." said Jason, and the players began tucking their flags into their belts.

I just want to win once! thought Austin, and he tucked his flag in too.

The Gators started out strong, making two touchdowns in the first half.

"Remember what I told you!" whispered Brice in the huddle.

Carson snapped the ball to Keiko. She lobbed it to Austin, and he took off down the field. On his left, a Gator came streaking toward Austin.

The Gator caught up with Austin at the five-yard line and grabbed for his flag, but it stayed tucked tightly in his belt.

"Touchdown!" yelled the referee as Austin crossed the goal line.

That night at dinner, Austin's dad smiled as he slapped an extra-big hamburger onto Austin's plate. "You must be hungry after that win!"

"I knew all your hard work would pay off," said Austin's mom.
"The Gators didn't pull a single Tiger flag!"

Suddenly, Austin wasn't very hungry.

Austin still had knots in his stomach as the Tigers warmed up for their next game. Everyone said the Mustangs were the best team in town.

"Great game last week, Tigers!" said Coach Lauren.

"But don't forget," added Coach Tony, "winning isn't the most important part of football."

Austin raised his hand. "My mom says the most important part is to have fun."

Coach Tony smiled. "Well, it's important to have fun, but it's even more important to play a game you can be proud of."

"That's right," said Coach Lauren. "If you've done your best and played fair, you can feel proud of every game, even the ones you lose."

"Don't forget to tuck in your flags!" said Brice as soon as the coaches left the huddle.

Austin crossed his arms.
"No," he said loudly.

Everyone looked at him.

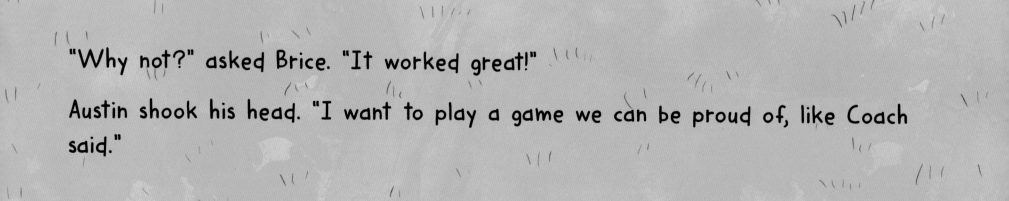

"Why not?" asked Brice. "It worked great!"

Austin shook his head. "I want to play a game we can be proud of, like Coach said."

The other
Tigers nodded.

"Me, too," said Jalen.

"No more cheating,"
said Carson.

Brice looked unhappy, but he didn't argue.

The Tigers played better than they ever had before.

With two minutes left
in the game, they needed just
one more touchdown to win fair and square!

Keiko dropped back to pass. The Mustangs were closing in fast.

Brice was wide open.
He jumped to catch her pass
and took off down the field!

Austin followed, blocking for him. Brice was almost to the goal line when a girl in a Mustang jersey cut in front of him.

The Mustang player yanked on Brice's flag, but it would not budge.

With a final burst of speed, Brice broke free and ran into the end zone, punching the air to celebrate the wining touchdown.

The Tigers rushed onto the field cheering, but Austin didn't feel like running anymore.

"Why so glum, Austin?" the referee asked.

Austin looked across the field at his teammates celebrating, and he took a deep breath. "I need to tell you something."

He knew why Brice had been able to score. He had cheated and tucked in his flag!

After the game,
Austin and his family went out for ice
cream. "I know it was probably hard for you
when the referee took away the touchdown,"
said Mom, "but we're so proud of you for being honest."

"We sure are," said Dad. "How do you feel?"

"Pretty good," said Austin, licking the drips from his chocolate cone.

"Even though you lost?" asked Dad.

Austin nodded. "It would have felt good to win, but it feels better to play fair."

He took another lick of ice cream and grinned. "And next time, we're going to do both!"

JOIN THE TEAM

THE TEAM DUNGY PICTURE BOOKS FOR
YOUNG READERS TEACH CHARACTER-BUILDING
LESSONS THROUGH THE WORLD OF SPORTS.

LOOK FOR MORE TEAM DUNGY BOOKS!

MARIA
FINDS COURAGE

A TEAM DUNGY STORY ABOUT SOCCER